Norfolk Public Library
Norfolk, NE

GETTING REAL STRATEGIES FOR TEENS IN NEED

I AM BEING CYBERBULLIED... WHAT'S NEXT?

C. R. MCKAY

NEW YORK

For Kathy Mahaney, whose life inspired so many small acts of kindness.

Published in 2022 by The Rosen Publishing Group, Inc.
29 East 21st Street, New York, NY 10010

Copyright © 2022 by The Rosen Publishing Group, Inc.

First Edition

Designer: Rachel Rising
Editor: Greg Roza

Portions of this work were originally authored by Caitie McAneney and published as *I Have Been Cyberbullied. Now What?* All new material in this edition was authored by C. R. McKay.

All rights reserved. No part of this book may be reproduced in any form without permission in writing from the publisher, except by a reviewer.

Cataloging-in-Publication Data

Names: McKay, C. R.
Title: I am being cyberbullied...what's next? / C. R. McKay.
Description: New York : Rosen Publishing, 2022. | Series: Getting real: strategies for teens in need
Identifiers: ISBN 9781499470567 (pbk.) | ISBN 9781499470574 (library bound) | ISBN 9781499470581 (ebook)
Subjects: LCSH: Cyberbullying--Juvenile literature. | Cyberbullying--Prevention--Juvenile literature.
Classification: LCC HV6773.15.C92 M35 2022 | DDC 302.34'3--dc23

Some of the images in this book illustrate individuals who are models. The depictions do not imply actual situations or events.

Manufactured in the United States of America

CPSIA Compliance Information: Batch #CSRYA22. For further information contact Rosen Publishing, New York, New York at 1-800-237-9932.

CONTENTS

INTRODUCTION 4

CHAPTER 1
WHAT IS CYBERBULLYING? 8

CHAPTER 2
PRIVATE LIFE ON BLAST 22

CHAPTER 3
THE REAL EFFECTS OF CYBERBULLYING 40

CHAPTER 4
THE LAW IS ON YOUR SIDE 58

CHAPTER 5
MOVING FORWARD AFTER CYBERBULLYING 66

CHAPTER 6
CREATING SAFE SPACES ONLINE 82

CONCLUSION 92

GLOSSARY 94

FOR MORE INFORMATION 96

FOR FURTHER READING 100

INDEX..102

ABOUT THE AUTHOR 104

INTRODUCTION

Imagine a bully who follows you home. Imagine a bully who sits in your room, sleeps by your bed, and gets into your head when no one else is around to defend you. Imagine a bully who can find you wherever you are, who can tear you down with hurtful comments without anyone around to witness it. This isn't just a made-up superbully—it's a cyberbully.

The rise of the internet has given people plenty of power. You can find almost anything online—facts for homework, new videos from YouTube stars and influencers, and all the hottest products. You can connect with friends and family on Facebook, share photographs on Instagram, post about what you're interested in on Tumblr, record music videos with TikTok, and document your day with Snapchat and YouTube. But the internet has also given us the power to bully from anywhere, anytime. Cyberbullying has become the ultimate power move, and its effects on victims can be devastating.

What is cyberbullying, anyway? Cyberbullying is threatening, harassing, or embarrassing someone through technology. Cyberbullies might use texting, social media posts, or direct messaging (DMing) to spread lies, forward another person's personal information or secrets, post cruel remarks, or harass and threaten others. And it's never been easier for bullies to reach people—more than 95 percent of

INTRODUCTION 5

Whether you use Instagram or TikTok, it's possible that cyberbullying might happen to you. Luckily, you can do things to protect yourself *before* the cyberbullying begins —and even while it's happening.

teens have access to a smartphone, and they spend an average of 7 hours on screens each day.

Internet activity makes up a huge chunk of many teens' social life. Therefore, victims may feel isolated as cyberbullying pollutes their online social life. It may feel as though they can't escape their bullies because the internet is *everywhere*. It only takes picking up a cell phone or logging into a school or home computer.

Cyberbullying and traditional bullying are closely related. If someone is a bully at school, they're more likely to be a bully online. Similarly, if someone is a victim at school, they're more likely to be a victim online. The internet is a wide-reaching tool—one that can allow bullies to have great control over their victims.

A 2018 Pew Research Study found that 59 percent of U.S. teens have experienced abusive online behaviors. These experiences (in order of their prevalence) include offensive name calling, spreading of false rumors, receiving unwelcome explicit pictures, constant "checking in" by someone other than a parent, receiving physical threats, and having their own explicit pictures shared without consent.

When they're caught or called out, cyberbullies may say their actions were a joke or not a big deal. But in reality, cyberbullying has serious effects on victims. This book explores why cyberbullying happens, as well as different forms of cyberbullying and its consequences. You'll also gain useful tools for preventing cyberbullying and getting help if it's happened to you or someone you know.

Contrary to how it might feel at the time, it is possible to recover from being cyberbullied and to move past the damage it might deal to your reputation. You can regain your online identity, your reputation, your safety, and your sense of self. Most importantly, you can learn to create safe spaces online and in your personal life—and develop resilience in the face of cyberbullying.

The internet is a wonderful invention! It allows us to do research, watch movies, play video games, and stay in touch with friends around the world. Unfortunately, it also allows bullies to harass their victims. Don't let this ruin the internet for you. This book will help.

CHAPTER 1

WHAT IS CYBERBULLYING?

Have you experienced cyberbullying in your own life? Have you cyberbullied another person? If you've ever been caught up in a cyberbullying situation, then you know that no two cases are the same. They exist across different social media platforms, in varying degrees of intensity. Some situations happen briefly, while others keep happening and become dangerous.

The Cyberbullying Research Center defines cyberbullying in the following way: "Cyberbullying is when someone repeatedly and intentionally harasses, mistreats, or makes fun of another person online or while using cell phones or other electronic devices."

In this chapter, we'll look at a few of the main types of cyberbullying. Equipping yourself with information is a great defense against cyberbullying. You can learn to identify cyberbullying behavior and keep yourself safe.

A COMMENT FOR EVERYTHING

Does it seem like everyone has a comment for *everything* these days? Most social media platforms allow comments on posts, including statuses, memes, pictures, and videos. While some comments might be positive, many are offensive or negative. And many are meant to cut a person down completely.

Posting mean comments is a common cyberbullying tactic. Dr. Justin Patchin at the Cyberbullying Research Center found posting mean comments was one of the most common forms of cyberbullying. The aim of posting these comments could be revenge, jealousy, or attention. Many times, the comments are used to build the cyberbully up—to make him or her feel better—while breaking the victim down. With a few keystrokes, cyberbullies can successfully get through to their victim, leaving the victim feeling powerless.

A 2019 study from the Cyberbullying Research Center found that nearly 1 in 4 teens had experienced a mean comment online in the last 30 days.

Mean comments are commonly seen on social networks. Platforms such as Instagram, Snapchat, and TikTok allow users to share photographs and videos of themselves, which makes them common places for this kind of cyberbullying. Platforms such as Facebook and Twitter allow users to write statuses and post comments to another person's profile, which is another tool for cyberbullies. The cyberbully can either create a hurtful post or comment on something a victim posts. Some offensive, hateful comments may be posted on a victim's social media page during an online fight. Posting these types of comments is sometimes called flaming.

Hurtful remarks come in many different forms. A common target for cyberbullying comments is a person's appearance—their height, weight, or any

When you post a picture online, you're probably hoping for positive comments or likes. When someone instead criticizes your appearance, it can be a big blow to your self-image.

WHO IS A VICTIM?

Cyberbullying victims don't ask to be bullied. So why do bullies seek them out? Each situation is vastly different, but there are a few factors that increase a person's chance of being cyberbullied.

Some victims are quick to get upset about things, which makes them more of a target. Bullies might enjoy getting a rise out of a victim who's easily provoked. They might think it's fun to watch the victim engage in an online fight. Provocative behavior might be more common for people who have ADHD (attention deficit hyperactivity disorder) or other disorders that affect a person's social behaviors or impulse control.

Passive people may also be more common victims because cyberbullies might think it's easier to get away with bullying that person.

Gender also affects cyberbullying situations. Girls are more likely to report that someone spread mean comments or rumors about them, while boys are more likely to report online threats.

difference that sets them apart from the societal "ideal." Cyberbullies often make hurtful remarks about people they see as weak or lesser in some way. That makes people with disabilities or special needs easy targets for cyberbullies. According to Dr. Marcia Eckerd in an article for Smart Kids with Learning Disabilities, people with learning and social disabilities, such as attention deficit disorder (ADD) and autism, are especially at risk for cyberbullying.

Mean comments may also call out a person's sexual orientation or gender identity. Cyberbullies often target people who are different from them, especially lesbian, gay, bisexual, transgender, and queer (LGBTQ+) individuals. In fact, according to a 2019 study by the Cyberbullying Reseach Center, the number of LGBTQ+ youths who have been cyber-

The Human Rights Campaign found that 73 percent of LGBTQ+ youth say they're more honest about their identities online than in real life. Because of this, it's especially important for these teens to find safe spaces online.

bullied is about 30 percent higher than the number of non-LGBTQ+ youths. Almost half of LGBTQ+ youths admit to being harassed or bullied online.

Whether a victim is gay or straight, a cyberbully might call attention to how many relationships a person has had, whether many or few. They may harass someone because of an alleged sexual act.

Hate groups recruit people, especially young white men, on comment boards like 4chan and social media sites. White supremacists and neo-Nazis encourage hate speech, violent threats, and slurs against minority groups, such as those with different religions, ethnicities, and sexual orientations.

Whether or not a person is different from the societal "norm" or majority, it's never the fault of a victim when they are targeted online with mean comments. Some people may say a person is "asking for criticism" when they post something or act a certain way, but that's a form of victim blaming. Mean comments are the problem—not the person they target.

THE WORLDWIDE RUMOR MILL

One of the most dangerous uses of the internet is to spread a rumor or lie. In person, it might take a while for a rumor or lie to go around a school or community. Online, the rumor or lie can spread like wildfire across a friend group, school, community, or the wider world.

According to a 2019 study performed by the Cyberbullying Research Center, more than 22 percent of youth admitted to being the victim of rumors online in the 30 days prior to the study. Of course, there were lies and rumors spread before the internet. Even now, this happens at school and in other public places. However, the internet is a different kind of place. It includes networks of people we know as well as those we don't know, and it reaches all over the world.

There are many kinds of lies and rumors a person might spread. They might make up something about a victim's dating history. They might spread a rumor about a girl being pregnant. They might even out someone for their sexual orientation or gender identity—a potentially damaging act that can never be undone. Rumors, whether they're founded in almost-truths or purely on lies, can be extremely damaging to the victim. They shape the way people treat the victim and interpret their words and actions. Rumors can pass from student to student and even on to teachers, employers, and family members.

Rumors and lies can be extremely damaging. They can hurt a victim's relationships and reputation and even the way the victim feels about themselves.

WHY DO BULLIES...BULLY?

There are many reasons why a person might bully. The American Psychological Association says that bullies may have negative beliefs and attitudes about others and themselves. Conflict might be a normal part of their home lives, and some have problems with school and home that they take out on others. One major factor is a lack of problem-solving and coping skills. They don't have the tools to deal with people in a healthy way. Bullies may have less empathy for others, or they may feel it is a way to stay popular or have power over others.

There are several factors that make people even more likely to cyberbully. The first is anonymity—people might feel they can say things behind a computer screen that they wouldn't say to someone's face. Some cyberbullies think their behavior is funny, and because they can't see the consequences of their actions (the way they hurt others), they don't think it's a big deal. Some are pressured by a group mentality, thinking they should join in on the cyberbullying or be left behind. Either way, cyberbullying gives wider power than in-person bullying. While in-person bullies might need to be bigger or stronger than their victims for intimidation, *anyone* can be a cyberbully.

16 | I AM BEING CYBERBULLIED...WHAT'S NEXT?

If someone spreads a picture of you—especially a "doctored" one—you might feel shocked and upset. You have the power to report the photograph and have it removed from social media.

A cyberbully can spread more than just words. To make people believe their lies, some cyberbullies spread pictures to support those lies or embarrass their victim. Picture-editing programs are available on any computer or phone. Many apps have the capability built in, so making a meme out of a person's picture is easy enough—and spreading it around is even easier. Today, cyberbullies can manipulate a picture to incriminate or embarrass a victim, even if this person has done nothing wrong. The cyberbully can spread these forged pictures or videos with their rumors as false evidence.

MYTHS AND FACTS:

- **MYTH #1**: Adults are well informed when cyberbullying happens.

- **FACT #1**: In fact, only 1 in 10 victims will tell a parent or trusted adult when cyberbullying happens to them. Around 60 percent of teens have witnessed bullying—but rarely intervene. Around 81 percent say that they *would* intervene if they could do so anonymously.

- **MYTH #2**: All social media platforms have an equal amount of cyberbullying.

- **FACT #2**: A 2017 survey by Ditch the Label found that 42 percent of Instagram users said they'd been harassed on the platform. Instagram was found to be the worst platform for cyberbullying, followed by Facebook (37 percent), Snapchat (32 percent), YouTube (10 percent), and Twitter (9 percent).

- **MYTH #3**: Cyberbullying isn't that big a deal—and it's not that common.

- **FACT #3**: A 2018 Pew Research Center study found that 59 percent of U.S. teens have been harassed or bullied online. That's nearly two-thirds of all teens in the nation!

WHO ARE YOU, REALLY?

Cyberbullies often get away with their behavior by hiding behind false identities. They can make up an account with a fake name or impersonate someone else with an account. In fact, in June 2019, Facebook removed 2.2 billion fake accounts in just one month!

Some people create profiles with fake names and pictures to fool people into thinking they're someone else. Some cyberbullies even hack, or break into, their victim's accounts and pretend to be them. They might use the victim's account to post things so everyone believes it was the victim, and not the bully, who did it.

False identities are a powerful and destructive tool for cyberbullies. They can hide behind made-up

WHAT IS CYBERBULLYING? 19

Some people "catfish" others to trick them and expose information that was given in secret (a cyberbullying tactic called trickery or outing). Other people want to get someone to like them.

personalities to harass someone without getting in trouble. But even worse, they can use a false identity to trick someone into trusting them. The victim may get emotionally attached to this person. In popular culture, this is informally called "catfishing."

The trend of catfishing inspired the MTV series *Catfish: The TV Show*, which first aired in 2012. People contact the show's host, Nev Shulman, when they or their loved ones believe they're being catfished. As a fellow victim of catfishing, Shulman listens to people who are being catfished and goes on a mission to find the truth. Often the truth is hard to find, and it's even harder to hear.

While some "catfish" are looking to lure people into online relationships with them, others are more dangerous. They want to lure people into violence.

In 2019, an Alaska teen killed her best friend after someone she met online promised her millions of dollars for the murder. The man catfished the teen girl, conning her into an online romance, and then asked for videos of her killing someone. This is an extreme example, but it illustrates the dangers of catfishing.

How can you spot a catfish or a false profile? The person will stay away from personal forms of communication, such as webcam chats or meeting in person. The person may have photographs that look like they haven't aged in years, talk about traumatic life events as an excuse for their elusive behavior, and be vague about their past or their personal connections.

Whenever you meet someone online, it's important to be aware of the dangers and be in open communication with a trusted adult about anything that makes you feel uncomfortable.

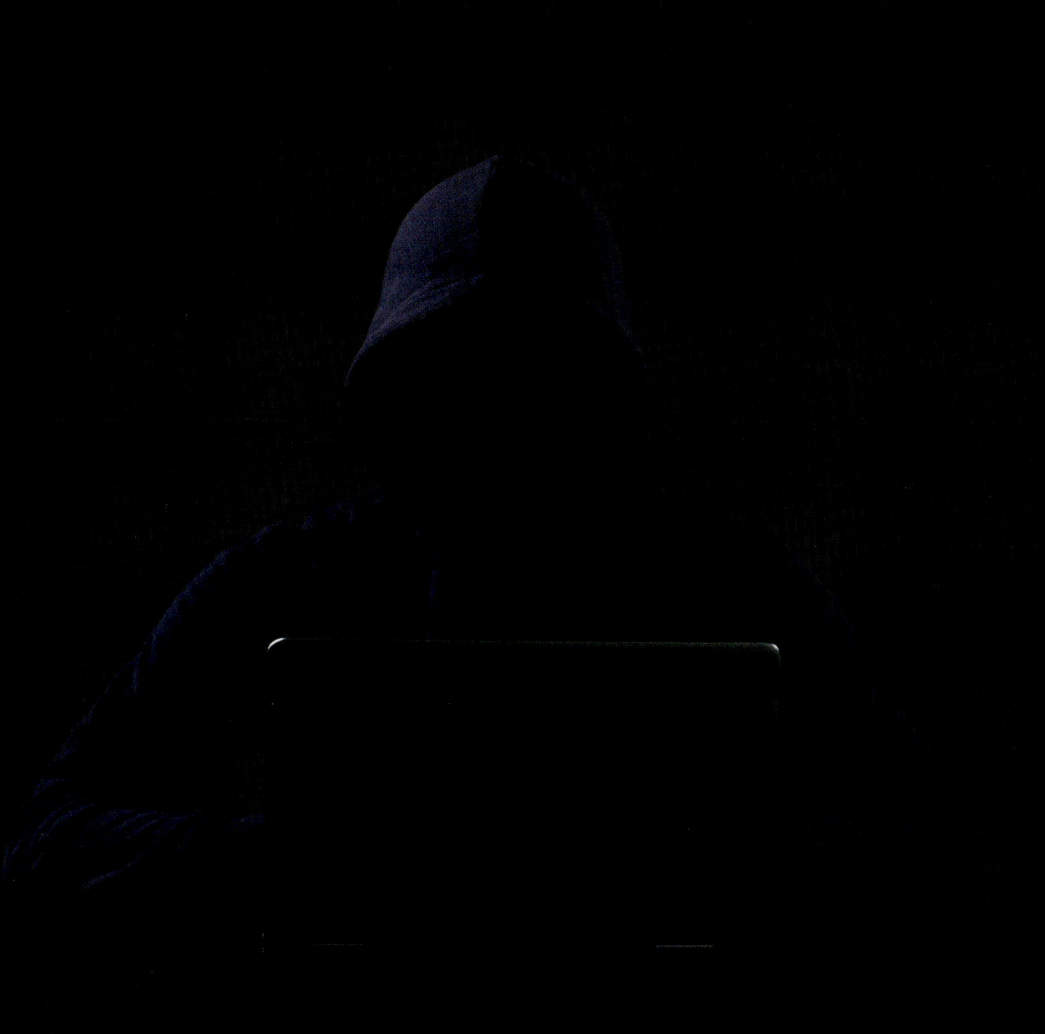

You never can really tell who you're speaking with online, especially when meeting new people. If anyone ever makes you feel uncomfortable online, tell a parent or another adult as soon as you can.

CHAPTER 2

PRIVATE LIFE ON BLAST

In the wrong hands, your information, private pictures and videos, and personal conversations can be used against you. In this chapter, we'll look at how to keep your information safe—and what can happen when it's not.

The internet is a trove of information. You can look up nearly anything—facts, figures, and yes, personal information about someone. So, what can you do to keep your private life *private*? And what happens when your private life is on blast for the world to see?

TAPPING INTO YOUR PERSONAL LIFE

How do cyberbullies get personal information? From hackers to ex-besties looking for revenge, your information is only as safe as the guards you put up against the people who might use your information against you. How can you keep your information safe and your pictures private? And how can those things be used against you?

KEEP YOUR INFORMATION SAFE!

The most important rule of sharing information online is this: Only share what you don't mind everyone seeing. You might think you're just sharing a funny selfie with a friend, but that friend might post it after you have a fight. You might think you're just expressing yourself by sharing your secrets with your friend group online—but that information can easily be leaked elsewhere.

You might trust your friends with your pictures—but you can't control how they use them if you have a fight.

Many people have had their private information or photographs leaked to the public when they've broken ties with someone they used to trust. This could be a best friend or a boyfriend or girlfriend. That person may have been a very caring person when you were friends or dating. However, after you cut ties, that person could take your information—racy pictures, private conversations, secrets—and share it online.

You may feel compelled to give information, pictures, and videos to someone you haven't even met. The internet makes it easy to connect with and open up to people you don't know. You may meet someone in a gaming community or on a social media website and establish a connection after only a short time. You might trust a person so much that you agree to give them private information or send them pictures and videos that you wouldn't want public.

The problem with interacting online is that you never know who you're actually talking to. People who use false identities to take information are often able to manipulate their victims into trusting them. They're often very smart too. They'll think of evidence they can use to prove they're the person they're pretending to be, such as pictures or accounts from other people. While you may see a picture of an attractive person your age, the person might be older and more dangerous. They might try to get you to trust them so they can ask you for your full name, school, address, phone number, or Social Security number. They might ask for explicit pictures or videos of you posing naked or in an incriminating position. Sometimes, these people aren't just cyberbullies—they're sexual predators.

To be safe, never give private information to anyone you don't know in person, and never send private pictures over the internet. Even if you do know the person, you want to be careful. If you're wondering if someone you're talking to online is actually the person you think they are, ask them about it in person (if you already know them) or over the telephone or a webcam.

HACKERS AND THIEVES

People don't always trick you into giving up your information—some take it without asking. It's good practice to never leave your accounts open or your devices unattended or unlocked. It's easy for people to log on and grab your information.

Someone can also steal information if you use a computer in a public place, such as a library. If you get up to talk to a teacher, a bully could get into your account and look for private pictures or messages. You may also be at risk of having your accounts hacked if you forget to log out of accounts on public computers.

To keep yourself safe, make sure to never leave your computer or phone unattended, especially in public places.

It's also possible for some people to access your digital information without even touching it. These people, called hackers, know how to use technology against people. Some hackers want your credit card or bank information so they can steal money or your identity. To keep yourself safe, never share credit card information—even if it's your family credit card—with anyone you don't know or with a company that doesn't seem reliable. There are many times you may need to enter credit card informa-

tion online, such as when you're buying an app or shopping, but make sure the websites are reputable. Many hackers break into your computer by spreading computer viruses and tracking cookies through programs you download.

Celebrities are at high risk for hackers because the hackers can sell pictures and incriminating information or spread them for attention. In 2014, a hacker released 500 celebrity photographs online, including racy pictures of actress Jennifer Lawrence. Other victims of celebrity photo hacks include Emma Watson, Scarlett Johansson, and Amanda Seyfried.

While some pictures or videos are just embarrassing, others can ruin your reputation.

LEAKED IMAGES

Pictures and videos are some of the most personal things that can be posted online. And when they are leaked, or spread without your consent, it can make you feel more vulnerable than ever.

Pictures can be used as visual evidence against you—evidence that you're not attractive, that you're clumsy, that you did something shameful. Most phones can also take videos, which can be even more incriminating as they can expose what you've done and said.

In the age of the internet, almost anyone is able to snap a picture or record a video at any time. Smartphones easily share images and videos via text, email, or social networks. Cyberbullies can use images to shred your self-esteem and give themselves power. Some cyberbullies may even use pictures as blackmail. There's a reason many people consider Instagram to be one of the worst platforms for cyberbullying, as it's completely image-based.

VIRAL EMBARRASSMENT

Embarrassing moments are a fact of life. They happen to everyone—tripping over something at school, messing up on stage, mispronouncing someone's name, or making other goofs. Embarrassing experiences can make your self-esteem plummet, but these moments are usually easy to recover from and even laugh about afterward.

But what if someone took a video of you doing something embarrassing? What if they snapped a picture when you fell in the hallway? Sometimes, embarrassing moments are captured and shared—and sometimes they even go viral.

Since many students have cell phones, it's common for them to take pictures and videos during their day. But that means no one is safe from having their picture taken and no moment can be completely private. Private conversations or interactions

LEAKED VIDEOS

Leaked videos of someone in a compromising position may seem funny at first. You're seeing someone with their guard down. However, posting these videos, or sharing them, can be more than just a joke—it can be a matter of life and death.

In 2014, a San Diego teen committed suicide after a video was leaked online. The video showed him in the most private of places—a bathroom. His classmates thought it was funny, and he was bullied both online and in person. The video went viral, affecting his school life and personal relationships. While some people probably shared the video just as a joke, it was very serious—serious enough to lead to someone's death.

can be spread around your school and around the internet in no time at all. Teens record videos of school fights, injustices they see, and time goofing around with their friends. But they also record pictures and videos of people being bullied or doing embarrassing things.

Bullying people at school is never OK. But when someone films the bullying and posts it online for others to see, it's also cyberbullying. The person who posts the video is no better than the bullies who harass someone at school.

Sometimes people post pictures to make others look unattractive, or they may take photos of someone doing something they wouldn't want others to see. Sometimes these moments go viral in the name of "harmless fun," but it's not comedy—often, it's a cruel form of cyberbullying.

Your online presence now could affect how college and job representatives see you in the future. A professional presence online can be ruined if wild party pictures surface.

PROOF OF PARTIES

Your reputation is something that you may have carefully constructed. Whether your goal is to go to college or get a great job after high school, then you probably have tried to work hard in school and give the impression that you're smart and capable. You want people to think of you as a dependable and trustworthy person.

Even the most dependable, intelligent person might let loose sometimes at a party, but pictures and videos of some moments could be damaging for their reputation. Not only can party pictures be embarrassing—they could get you in major trouble.

Parties are places to be especially careful, as you never know who's watching you from across the room or taking pictures and videos. And with many people nearby, there are many opportunities to do or say something embarrassing or make bad decisions. You might get into an argument with someone. You might decide to drink alcohol or experiment with drugs. Drinking and drugs will further impair your judgment, which could result in poorer decision-making.

If you're drinking, doing drugs, or participating in any other illegal activity, such as vandalism, pictures and videos can be the evidence that gets you in trouble. These pictures and videos might be shared online or used as blackmail. They could have serious consequences depending on the nature of your partying activities, including being grounded by your parents, suspended from school, or punished by the law.

Being under the influence of drugs or alcohol might make you a target for bullies who think the way you're acting or speaking is funny. This can quickly spiral out of control. There are things you can do to make sure you stay out of this sort of picture. Don't go to any party that you're not allowed to go to. Make sure your parents know where you are and who you're hanging out with. If you do go to a party, don't participate in vandalism or underage drinking or drugs.

In the age of smartphones and an eager internet audience, you have to be careful about your reputation at all times—even at parties. Act in the way

PRIVATE LIFE ON BLAST

Some teens might think taking pictures of themselves and their friends drinking alcohol is funny or cool. But the images can have a negative impact on their future.

An April 2019 study by the Cyberbullying Research Center found that 14 percent of teens had sent explicit messages and 23 percent had received them.

you want the world to see you. However, if someone does post a picture or video of you that is damaging, it's best to reach out to a trusted adult to speak about it honestly. Cyberbullying doesn't have to be a secret burden hidden behind a veil of shame.

THE MOST PRIVATE OF IMAGES

Pictures and videos with sexual content are probably the ones you regard as most private. These images might show a person either partially naked, completely naked, or in a sexually suggestive position. These images can be used to ruin someone's reputation, hurt their feelings, or even put them in unsafe positions with sexual predators.

Many social networking websites have rules

against such images, but that doesn't stop people from posting them. Once a cyberbully obtains a sexual image of their victim, they can easily post it to a number of sites, and they may not be stopped until it's spread to a wide audience.

How do cyberbullies get sexual images from their victims? Some hackers leak photographs or videos obtained illegally. Other online predators find sexual images of young people and share them. But many sexual images are given to someone by the victim themselves—through sexting.

Sexting is sending or receiving sexually suggestive images, usually by cell phone. Some teens see this behavior as normal. They may want to show off their bodies because they're proud of them. They may want to send a crush or significant other a picture—whether it was asked for or not. Some teens are pressured for pictures by people they meet online or people they know well and feel connected to.

However normal sexting may seem, it does come with risks. Even if you're in a relationship with someone, they may share your images when you break up. This is called "revenge porn." If you're sharing the images with someone you've never met online, they could be posting your images to online communities of sexual predators. Sharing sexual images of someone under the age of 18 is often considered child pornography.

Once you've sent a photo to someone, you can't control where it goes. It could wind up in the hands of strangers, including predators.

CHAPTER 3

THE REAL EFFECTS OF CYBERBULLYING

Some cyberbullies behave in ways they wouldn't in person because they can't see all the consequences of their actions. They can't see the deflated look of a person who has just been teased. They can't see the tears of the person who has been dragged through the rumor mill. It's all good fun—or is it?

Cyberbullying has serious effects on the psychological and social well-being of its victims, from depression and anxiety to substance abuse and eating disorders.

In this chapter, advice from licensed clinical mental health counselor Nicole Newcomb-Chumsky will give you the tools you need to help identify the consequences of cyberbullying and the coping skills you need to move past the digital warfare.

A BLOW TO YOUR SOCIAL LIFE

A person's social life takes place in a variety of environments—schools, homes, and local hangouts. However, many people have an online social life that includes everyone they know in one place. It's important to remember that what you say online can affect your reputation—in both positive and negative ways.

A person's reputation consists of the thoughts, beliefs, and feelings that other people have about them. Someone might gain a negative reputation through no fault of their own. Cyberbullying can take someone's reputation from positive to negative quickly.

Nicole Newcomb-Chumsky says, "Cyberbullying changes social standing depending on how severe the bullying, how many people are partaking in supporting the bully, and how the victim handles it."

When someone is bullied, they may have a group of friends to support them. The more people on a person's side, the more support they might feel they have. As in traditional bullying, having a support system can help a victim feel protected from harm. However, the more people involved in the bullying—a

A victim's social circle can shrink until that person feels isolated from those around them.

whole class, a wide-ranging Facebook group—the worse a person's social standing may suffer.

A person's social standing also depends on how they feel about the situation. Newcomb-Chumsky says, "More times than not, the victim will perceive their standing as being lowered simply because they're embarrassed and anticipate a change in social status." Acting embarrassed, aggressive, or overly defensive can reinforce a negative reputation. It can make the victim isolate himself or herself before others can do it. If a victim handles the situation with positivity and grace, their reputation might stay about the same.

This can be a hard line to walk—how do you act gracefully to a comment that has cut you to the core? It takes important coping tools to deal with the emotions you may feel as a victim of cyberbullying.

A SHOT TO YOUR SELF-ESTEEM

Especially in your teen years, your self-esteem is probably greatly affected by what people think about you. A person's self-esteem is their confidence in their own abilities and worth. Self-esteem can be affected by a person's thoughts about their intelligence, physical attractiveness, and social standing. When people around you criticize you, your outlook on yourself can change dramatically.

Drs. Patchin and Hinduja found in their 2010 study for the *Journal of School Health* that there's a significant relationship between low self-esteem and experiences with cyberbullying. And the more severe the bullying—from annoying to threatening—the more of an impact they can have on a person's self-esteem.

Newcomb-Chumsky notes the difference between traditional bullying and cyberbullying and why cyberbullying can be worse for one's self-esteem. "The ability to cyberbully has increased the frequency and intensity of the verbal and emotional abuse. As a result, one's self-esteem is exposed to attacks more often and requires a higher level of confidence to defend itself. Typically, an individual's self-esteem is not prepared for this level of harassment."

A person's self-esteem is often related to how they feel about their appearance or their body image. One person might think they're too short, while another may think they're overweight. Having a low self-image can result in various issues, including anxiety, depression, or eating disorders such as anorexia and bulimia.

People with anorexia may hold the food they eat to very unhealthy standards, or they may eat a lot and then make up for it by not eating, vomiting, or exercising too much. Their weight reaches less than 85 percent of what's considered normal for their height and age.

Cyberbullying can play a part in a person's body image, and in some cases, can lead to eating disorders. Newcomb-Chumsky says, "Something as little as hearing a peer talk about their clothing size and calories can lead a teenager to feel inadequate

If a cyberbully posts unflattering pictures of a person or comments about their weight or looks, a victim's body image can go from positive to negative, or worsen greatly.

and start assessing their weight. The pressure compounds once bullying is introduced."

However, Newcomb-Chumsky stresses that often many things need to fall into place for an eating disorder to manifest, such as a family history of eating disorders, a tendency to strive toward perfection, anxiety, or other trauma.

A 2018 study from the Department of Social Psychology at the University of Málaga (Spain) found that people with greater emotional intelligence and self-esteem were less likely to be victims of cyberbullying. Building your self-esteem may help you recover from cyberbullying attacks—and keep them from happening in the future.

BULLYING TAKES A MENTAL TOLL

The sick feeling you get when you log into your Instagram. The sadness you feel when someone uses hateful words against you in your DMs. The fear you feel when you think of posting a picture online.

These are all examples of the ways cyberbullying can affect your mental health. The mental toll of cyberbullying can be extremely damaging to victims in many different ways.

ADDING TO ANXIETY

We all feel anxiety from time to time—that undeniable reaction to stress that seems to take over the body and mind. This feeling of fear, nerves, or outright panic makes some people avoid certain situations, people, or objects.

Social anxiety is stress that comes from being around certain people in certain situations. Cyberbullying can heighten a person's social anxiety, leading them to actively avoid those situations or feel extreme stress in public places such as school.

Victims of cyberbullying may feel self-conscious around their peers, always on guard both online and in person.

Newcomb-Chumsky comments, "Teens already think that people are always looking at them and judging. Cyberbullying confirms these beliefs and consequently increases anxiety that creates a preoccupation with one's inadequacies." Imagine walking down your school hallway after seeing a bully post something about you online. You might feel as if people are staring and whispering about you—whether they are or not. "If someone is already struggling with social anxiety, then it becomes exacerbated,"

Newcomb-Chumsky adds. In other words, cyberbullying just adds to the anxiety you might feel in everyday life, turning it up a notch and affecting your relationships with others.

DEEPENING DEPRESSION

Have you ever gone through a long period of extreme sadness? This could be major depression, and in 2019, the National Institutes of Health estimated that 3.2 million teens had suffered a major depressive episode in the past year. People who suffer from depression may find it hard to enjoy activities they used to enjoy, and they may even find it hard to sleep, eat, concentrate, or communicate with others.

A 2015 study by JAMA Pediatrics found a consistent relationship between cyberbullying and depression. As with anxiety and eating disorders, depression happens because of a number of factors, including family history with depression, lack of support, and trauma. However, cyberbullying can take someone with preexisting depression and make it even worse. Newcomb-Chumsky says, "If consistent, [cyberbullying] can lead to long-lasting emotional problems. If an individual is already experiencing other risk factors for depression, then cyberbullying can definitely be the straw that breaks the camel's back."

If you're a victim of cyberbullying who suddenly feels sad for prolonged periods of time, and you feel unable to live the way you used to, you may have depression. If you suddenly feel nervous or fearful of social situations in a way that interferes with learning or relating to others, you may have anxiety. Tell a parent, doctor, or other trusted adult if you feel this way. Dealing with your feelings early on can keep you from developing harmful behaviors, such as substance abuse and self-harm. These mental health issues can be helped with the right resources and support, which will be further discussed in Chapter 5.

A MATTER OF LIFE AND DEATH

Some cases of cyberbullying, coupled with a person's existing anxiety and depression, may be a matter of life and death. Behaviors such as substance abuse, self-harm, and even suicide may occur, depending on the frequency and severity of the bullying, the number or influence of the bullies, and the victim's support system.

SELF-HARM

Self-harm, also known as self-injury or self-directed violence, is a behavior in which people intentionally cause harm to themselves. Most self-harm behaviors are known clinically as "non-suicidal self-injury," because they're not intended to cause suicide.

However, accidental deaths do occur with some self-harm behaviors, such as cutting. These behaviors affect a large portion of the teenage population; in fact, as many as one in four teenage girls does this. For someone who is being cyberbullied—and already dealing with mental health issues—self-harm might be a way to deal with the torment.

Newcomb-Chumsky comments, "Bullying does not directly lead to self-harm. However, it does have a significant impact if other risk factors are present or if self-harming has occurred previously." There are many ways that people can harm themselves if they're feeling emotional distress. They may starve themselves or isolate themselves from others. They may take a more active route and bang their head against things or burn themselves. Some people cut themselves with sharp objects.

Cutting, like other forms of self-harm, is a way that some young people cope with their feelings. It often brings a sense of control and relief, putting physical pain in the place of mental pain. Many young people hide their self-harm from others by hurting themselves in ways and in places that no one else can see. That makes it hard to get accurate statistics about self-harm. Some young people get their ideas of self-harm from websites that promote it, which can be dangerous and life-threatening. These websites, like cyberbullying, are just another way that young people can suffer because of irresponsible online content.

TikTok has been linked to broadcasted suicides, self-harm events, and deadly "challenges"—an awful by-product of dangerous online communities.

CYBER SELF-HARM

What if someone cyberbullies themselves? Cyber self-harm, also called digital self-harm, involves emotional injury instead of physical injury. A person might post mean or hurtful comments about themselves, either in private or in a public forum or on social media.

A 2017 survey in the *Journal of Adolescent Health* found that 6 percent of teens had anonymously posted negative comments about themselves.

Cyber self-harm was likely involved in the death of Hannah Smith, a teenager who committed suicide in 2014 after receiving multiple messages telling her that she should kill herself. After she committed suicide, an investigation was started into the source of these tormenting emails, only to find that 98 percent of them were sent from her own computer.

Why would teens post something negative about themselves? It might be a way to give self-hatred an audience, or it might be a cry for help with anxiety or depression. It may be a way to get attention from peers or to have negative commentary noticed and replaced with compliments and support. It could be a way to validate insecurities. Surprisingly, boys engaged in cyber self-harm more than girls—perhaps because they didn't feel able to be open about their insecurities.

SUBSTANCE ABUSE

Substance abuse is a form of self-harm that, unfortunately, is sometimes seen as acceptable or "cool" in the confines of high school. Substance abuse is repeatedly using drugs, such as alcohol, pain pills, marijuana, and narcotics. A person who uses these

Abusing drugs and alcohol can lead to a long list of physical and mental health issues. In some severe cases, substance abuse can lead to overdose and sometimes death.

substances often becomes dependent on them over time. They may feel they need that drug in order to feel normal.

According to The National Center on Addiction and Substance Abuse at Columbia University, American teenagers who spend time on social media sites are at an increased risk of smoking, drinking, and drug use. They also found that teens who have been cyberbullied are more than twice as likely to use tobacco, alcohol, and marijuana than teens who have not been cyberbullied.

Why do some victims turn to drugs? One reason is that drugs sometimes offer the kind of mental escape that victims are looking for. It's a way—a dangerous way—of trying to escape the real world temporarily. Some victims might do drugs to try to fit in with a social group or make themselves look cool. Others might do it as a cry for help.

SUICIDAL THOUGHTS

Youth suicides are on the rise in the United States. According to 2017 data from the National Center for Health Statistics and the Centers for Disease Control and Prevention, suicide was the second leading cause of death among teenagers and young adults ages 15 to 24. Nearly 10.6 deaths per 100,000 youths were recorded that year—a record high. Could the internet and cyberbullying have contributed to the sharp increase in suicides and suicide attempts?

In 2010, Drs. Patchin and Hinduja researched the correlations between bullying experiences and thoughts of suicide. They found that young people who experienced cyberbullying—either as the bully or victim—had more suicidal thoughts and were more likely to attempt suicide than those who weren't involved. They also found that victims were more likely to have suicidal thoughts than the bullies.

Why would someone resort to taking their own life? The answer is complicated. Newcomb-Chumsky

To many people who are victims of cyberbullying, it can seem like there's no way out. This can lead to suicidal thoughts. However, there's always hope for those who need it.

says, "Suicide is not an overnight decision and like eating disorders, has many precipitating factors. By the time that a suicide has occurred, there have already been many unsuccessful attempts at coping by the individual." We all have ways of coping with emotional distress, such as reaching out to a friend or family member, listening to favorite music, or writing in a journal. However, some people who suffer from depression and anxiety may find that none of their coping skills are working to make them feel better, which can make them feel hopeless. "At the point of committing the suicide, the victim genuinely feels there is no other way out of their suffering," Newcomb-Chumsky adds.

Unfortunately, there have been many suicide cases linked to cyberbullying. While it's sometimes unclear if cyberbullying was the biggest reason for each suicide, these severe cases show how cyberbullying can traumatize a person until they feel there's no other way out. They may feel that the ridicule will never stop, that the lies and rumors spread about them will continue to spread, and that there's nowhere that's safe.

Some cyberbullies even pressure victims to kill themselves, as in the case of the 2014 death of Conrad Roy III. The Massachusetts teen was relentlessly pressured to kill himself through texts by his girlfriend, Michelle Carter.

If you or anyone you know is having thoughts about suicide, contact the National Suicide Prevention Lifeline at 1-800-273-TALK (1-800-273-8255).

Though it may not feel like it, there's always another way to solve a problem, to fix your reputation and sense of self, and to find meaningful relationships despite cyberbullying.

The National Suicide Prevention Lifeline offers other resources for people at risk. You can call the number for immediate help. Visit their website for more information: suicidepreventionlifeline.org.

CHAPTER 4

THE LAW IS ON YOUR SIDE

There's an important thing to remember if you've been cyberbullied—it's never your fault. Everyone has the right to safety on the internet and in real life. There are laws and rules in place to keep you safe and stop the cyberbullying attacks.

Most cyberbullying cases are brought to justice under harassment, sexting, and discrimination laws. Currently, there are no federal laws directed at bullying, though that may change in the future. States and local governments have laws, rules, and regulations that might help you. Get familiar with your local laws and the rules and regulations put in place by your own school. Knowing your rights can help you get the upper hand in a cyberbullying situation.

LET'S LOOK AT LAWS

So, you've been cyberbullied. Do you have a legal case against your attacker? First, ask yourself a few questions: Did the cyberbully attack you once with a mean comment that you could shrug off—or was it a string of attacks that were very serious? Threatening messages and repeated damaging remarks can fall under harassment or cyberharassment laws.

Most states have laws against cyberstalking and cyberharassment, which are included under traditional stalking and harassment umbrellas. Because of the increase in cyberbullying, all but a few states have criminal sanctions on cyberbullying or electronic harassment.

Some cyberbullying situations may be based on discrimination. Discrimination means treating someone a certain way because of their race, sex, gender, disability, sexual orientation, national origin, or religion. Since many cyberbullies torment those who are different from them, many cases may fall

Cyberbullies may use slurs, or offensive names, on social media when they might not say them in person.

under discriminatory harassment laws. According to Stopbullying.gov, discriminatory harassment is illegal under federal law, so federally funded schools are required by law to take care of a bullying situation based on discrimination.

Cyberbullying against minority groups may also be classified as a hate crime, or "cyberhate." Hate crimes are very serious. In 2009, President Obama signed into law the Matthew Shepard and James Byrd Jr. Hate Crimes Prevention Act. The act made it a federal crime to willfully cause bodily injury (or to attempt to do so using a dangerous weapon) because of the victim's actual or perceived race, color, religion, national origin, sexual orientation, or gender identity. While cyberbullying doesn't usually cause bodily injury, cyberhate crimes are still serious.

Severe cyberbullying cases can be labeled as cyberstalking. Cyberstalking is extremely dangerous, as it demonstrates a bully or predator's intent to harm another person. In these cases, a person uses the internet to stalk someone, which shows a serious threat to a victim's safety. A victim may try blocking or avoiding the cyberstalker, but the cyberstalker may find and bother them again.

In many cases, cyberstalkers can be charged with a misdemeanor or felony. In 2018, two 12-year-old girls from Florida were charged with stalking a fellow student who killed herself because of their actions. Cyberbullying laws played a large role in the stalking case.

SEXTING, CHILD PORNOGRAPHY, AND SEXTORTION

If someone is distributing sexual pictures of you, the case might fall under state laws about child pornography and sexting. Child pornography is any sexual picture or video that's taken of a minor, or a young person under the age of 18. Some states have sexting laws and some don't. The ones that don't may default to child pornography laws, so punishment in those places may be more severe.

In 2017, a 22-year-old New Hampshire man pled guilty to a massive sextortion scheme. "Sextortion" means blackmailing people to send sexual pictures over the internet. The man would force girls to send him sexual pictures or would hack into their accounts to find them. His constant harassment put his victims in a tough place—some were even afraid to come forward. Because they did, however, the man was charged and sent to prison.

The Cyberbullying Research Center examined sextortion in a 2019 study, finding that 43 percent of victims said their attacker had threatened to send the picture to their friends, 29 percent said the attacker threatened to send the picture to their parents, and 35 percent were threatened with their picture being shared online.

READING UP ON RULES

As a citizen of the United States and a student at your school, you have rights. You have the right to education. You have the right to learn, play, and participate in school activities in a way that's fair

Schools have to address bullying when it makes the school a violent, unsafe, or unhealthy place for a person to learn or participate in activities.

and safe. When cyberbullying interferes with these rights, it's important to report the bullying to your school. Your school may have rules and regulations in place for this kind of abuse.

By law, schools have the responsibility to address bullying behavior, especially if it's severe, happening repeatedly, or tormenting a student so badly they can't learn. Cyberbullying must also be addressed if it's based on discrimination of race, color, national origin, sex, disability, or religion.

While all schools need to address bullying of these kinds, each school may have its own bullying and cyberbullying policies. Check your school's guidebook or website to find out what its rules and regulations are. Some schools may have special rules about misuse of social networking for teasing and making rude remarks. Other schools may have regulations that limit the use of in-school internet.

Each school has its own way of dealing with bullies, both traditional and cyber. But in general, all schools are expected to look into a cyberbullying complaint and question those involved without bias. They usually interview students involved, obtain written statements, and communicate with the students about ending the bullying. The school should also follow up with the affected students, especially the victim, to see if the cyberbullying is continuing or has stopped. The school should try to prevent future cyberbullying cases by bringing awareness of its bullying policy to the school community.

Cyberbullying can happen anywhere. It's important to educate yourself and others about the rules and regulations of your school. It's also important to be familiar with the rules of places you might take part in programs outside school, including dance studios or martial arts schools.

Some people are afraid to come forward when cyberbullying happens to them. They don't want to testify against others, or they might believe people won't take them seriously. But laws and rules are put in place to keep you safe. Above all, the rules and regulations of your community, school, or extracurricular activities should help you to feel as if your voice is important.

It's important to remember that there's always help for victims of cyberbullying. If you're afraid to talk to your parents, you may have a favorite teacher or counselor you can talk to at school. You'll learn more about your options in the next chapter.

CHAPTER 5

MOVING FORWARD AFTER CYBERBULLYING

Cyberbullying may be one of the hardest things you've ever had to deal with. But it's important to remember that you can still move forward. Recovering from a traumatic event like a severe cyberbullying attack may seem impossible, but with the right coping skills, you can get your life back.

This chapter will cover some essential tools for dealing with trauma and negative emotions. You may need additional help from a trusted adult or a therapist to regain your balance—and there's no shame in reaching out. Making the right moves after being cyberbullied can help you recover mentally and emotionally and gain justice. They can also keep you safe from future attacks.

YOU ARE NOT ALONE

Having a strong support system is essential to our emotional well-being—especially in times of crisis. You need to know that there are people on your side, people you can talk to and who will help you resolve a problem. Who are the people in your life who support you? They might be parents, guardians, family, or friends. If you don't yet have a strong support system, reaching out to teachers, coaches, or counselors is a good start.

If you're being cyberbullied in a persistent, severe way, it's important to let your parents or guardians know about it. If the cyberbullying is harsh enough, they may try to contact your school or legal authorities to seek justice for you or at least

There's no shame in going to therapy. Therapists, counselors, or psychologists can help you through talk therapy. Doctors, psychologists, and psychiatrists might prescribe medication in addition to talk therapy, if your depression or anxiety is severe.

stop future cyberbullying from happening. If you're very upset, they may find you a school counselor or other licensed therapist to talk to, which will help you work through your negative feelings.

Some young people are afraid that if they tell their parents about cyberbullying, their parents will take away their internet privileges. If much of your social life exists online, this may seem like a worse punishment than the cyberbullying. If there are pictures or posts that are being spread around that you're not proud of, you may be afraid your parents will be upset with you. This happens in many cases of young people who have sexual or party images shared. However, it's important to know that, in most cases, your parents or guardians have your best interests in mind.

If cyberbullying is happening between you and another classmate, or if you witness it happening, you should tell a teacher or school counselor. It's their responsibility to make the school a safe and healthy place to learn. Your teacher, school counselor, or principal might investigate the cyberbullying, talk to everyone involved to get the full story, and then deal with the situation the way they see fit. Many victims are afraid to come forward because they may feel that doing so would be embarrassing and bring attention to the situation. However, if the cyberbullying keeps happening and becomes damaging, it may be necessary.

If you don't feel comfortable talking to a parent or teacher, you can always talk to a therapist. Anything you say to a therapist is confidential, unless it involves the threat of serious harm to you or another young person. As a mental health therapist, Nicole Newcomb-Chumsky recommends therapy to deal with cyberbullying. She says, "An experienced therapist can guide an individual through processing their thoughts, feelings, and past experiences so the victim can make sense of it, learn how to cope in a healthy way, and work toward bettering their future interactions with peers."

10 QUESTIONS TO ASK A THERAPIST

1. What does healthy online behavior look like?
2. Are my online relationships and friendships safe?
3. Are there any teen support groups in my area?
4. How can I cope with anxiety and depression?
5. What are some tools I can use to calm down when I feel overwhelmed or attacked?
6. What can I do to help my self-esteem?
7. How can I express myself online without fear of being judged?
8. What interpersonal skills can I use when faced with cyberbullies and other difficult people?
9. How can I create a support system for moments of crisis?
10. How can I talk to my parents about cyberbullying without feeling ashamed of my online behavior?

Remember—you're not alone. Many people have been through something similar. Taylor Swift opened up about being cyberbullied online. She was called names, criticized, and harassed. On her famous *Reputation* tour in 2018, Swift told a Phoenix audi-

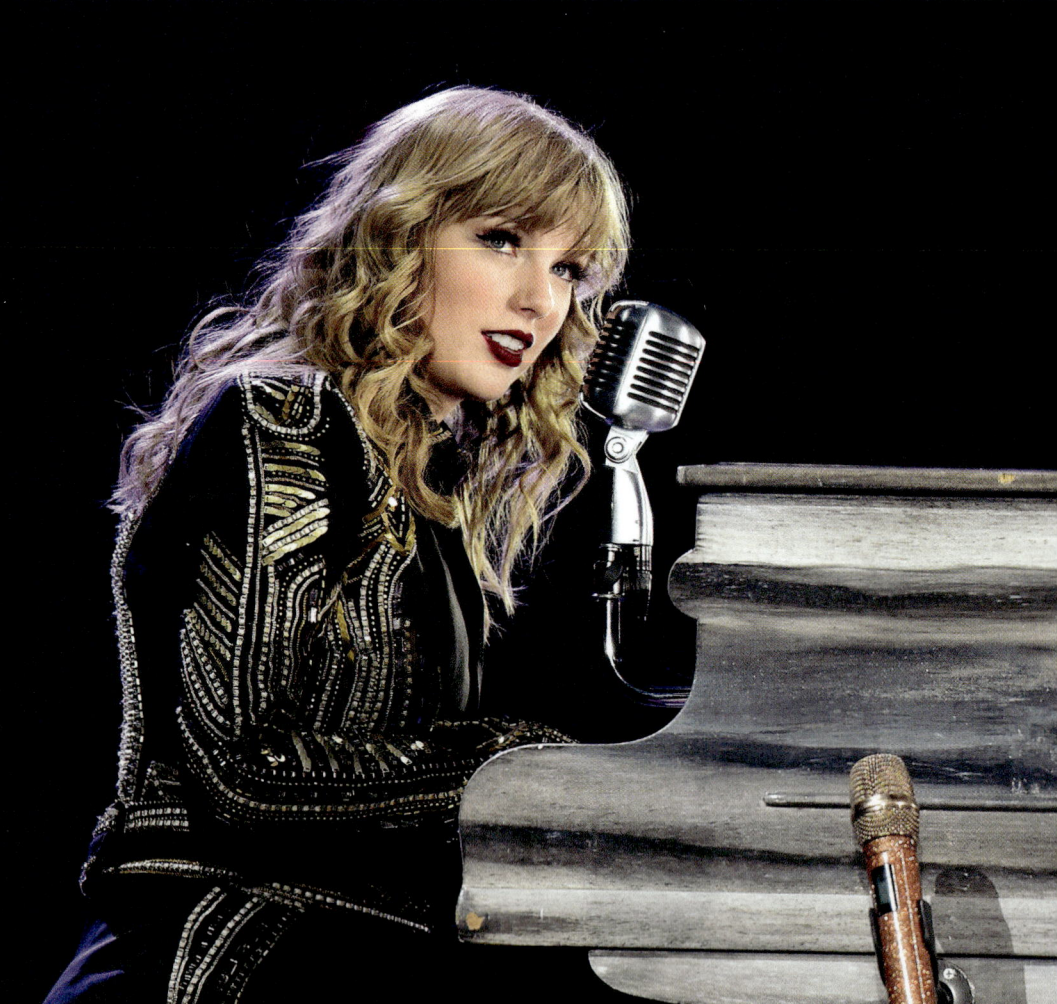

Taylor Swift said, "I think the lesson is that you shouldn't care so much if you feel misunderstood by a lot of people who don't know you, as long as you feel understood by the people who do know you."

MOVING FORWARD AFTER CYBERBULLYING

ence, "I went through some times when I didn't know if I was going to get to do this anymore. I wanted to send a message to you guys that if someone uses name-calling to bully you on social media, and even if a lot of people jump on board with it, that doesn't have to beat you. It can strengthen you instead."

DEVELOPING COPING SKILLS

Recovery may not happen overnight. It takes work for negative emotions and feelings to subside. But in time, you will be able to move on.

What coping skills can you use to recover from cyberbullying? First, you can engage in positive self-talk. That means thinking positive things about yourself. With cyberbullying, the negativity sometimes seems overwhelming, causing your self-esteem to plummet. The way to counter those negative thoughts is with positive thoughts about yourself. What are your strengths? What are you good at? What do you like about yourself? These positive things can help fight against the negative comments from others.

Radical acceptance is another coping skill. Radical acceptance means accepting yourself, others, and

Finding your breath through meditation is something you can control in the middle of a chaotic cyberbullying situation.

the situation around you. It means looking at a situation and observing it without getting caught up in it or passing judgment. You don't have to agree with what's going on, but you can still accept it. Instead of thinking, *that embarrassing photo is public and I can't stand it,* you could think, *there's a photo of me out in the public. I accept that and I'm moving past it.* Radical acceptance is a difficult skill to master, but it can help you in many situations in life.

It's also important to accept what you're feeling. If you're feeling depressed and isolated, accept that you're feeling that way, and that it's OK. Feeling sad over losing friends or being bullied is a normal reaction. Be patient with yourself as you work through these feelings. Telling yourself that it's not normal to be upset will only drive you deeper into depression. Similarly, if you're feeling anxious, accept that anxiety. Remind yourself that it's normal to feel nervous in school if you're being cyberbullied. It's normal to fear that people might not like you. Accept these feelings, be patient with them as they run their course, and work towards more positive feelings in the future.

Meditation often helps people accept what's going on in their life and calm down. People tend to react right away when something bad happens. Instead,

REPUTATION REPAIR

Cyberbullying can harm your reputation so badly that you might think all is lost. However, you can repair your reputation by using effective interpersonal skills.

The first thing to remember is that many times, if you don't engage with a bully or act aggressively towards them, the situation will eventually fizzle out. It may take a few weeks or months, but many times, the talk of the day becomes forgotten over time.

Acting with a positive attitude and having positive interactions with people will also help rebuild your reputation. Try your best to think and act rationally in the face of cyberbullying and show people that you can handle negativity without turning into a negative person.

To rebuild your reputation online, you can delete any old accounts associated with cyberbullying and create new accounts with advanced privacy settings. Let your online identity be one of positivity and friendliness, and resist the urge to over-share or to engage in drama online.

If you need to take a total break from social media for a while, that's always an option. Going "off the grid" can help you foster more important relationships in person.

take some time to breathe and meditate. Breathe in for four counts and out for six. Close your eyes and turn inward. You might visualize a calm moment or place, or you might repeat a helpful mantra. Doing yoga or going for a walk or jog may also calm you down. Once you are calm, you can react to a situation with a more appropriate response. Slowing down and reflecting helps you realize that you are in con-

There are numerous ways to cope with negative emotions and anxiety. Taking a walk or jog will help blow off steam and focus your thoughts. Studies show spending time with pets can also reduce stress.

76 | I AM BEING CYBERBULLIED...WHAT'S NEXT?

Spending quality time with friends and others close to you, in person rather than on the internet, is a great way to lift your spirits and improve your self-esteem.

trol of your thoughts, feelings, and actions.

GET OUTSIDE!

The internet might seem like it invades every part of your life. You probably carry your phone with you, so it's always available. It's good to remember that there is a world apart from the internet.

Unplug from your phone and laptop and spend time with your friends in the real world. While you may feel you have many friends on social media and gaming communities, you can also build and grow friendships in the real world that mean more.

How can you nurture your friendships outside of the internet? Instead of texting or DMing your friends, make plans to hang out with them after school or on the weekends. Face-to-face time with your friends may help you forget about the cyberbullying you face online and can show you that there's more to the world than hurtful comments and rumors. If you feel that you don't have many friends in the real world, make an effort to meet new people by joining a club, activity, or volunteer project.

Whether you love sports, art, or anything else, there's a club for it! These activities can do more than just help you gain a great circle of real-world friends. They can help you find your passion for something you're good at. If you like art, spending a few hours a day painting can help you forget about cyberdrama and focus on creating something. If you like music, learning how to play the piano can help you focus on expressing yourself through music. It's important to make

Athletics and team sports can help you beat depression and anxiety. Exercise is good for your body as well as your mind. Sports are also a great way to make friends with similar interests.

a life for yourself outside of the space where you were bullied.

What if you see your cyberbullies in real life? While some may go away once you're disconnected from the internet, others may be sitting next to you in class or see you in the hallway. First, try to avoid them. Walk a different way in the hallway or sit away from them in class. If they come after you, try not to engage with them. Don't let what they say bother you. And if it does, try not to show it. If they keep it up, report it.

Building a greater life outside of the internet can help you see what's important—real friends, laughter, and fun—instead of the number of likes or negative comments you get on a picture or post. The real world is full of opportunities for connection, and all you have to do is unplug.

Unplugging from the internet might be a tough thing to do, but you may be very glad you did it.

CHAPTER 6

CREATING SAFE SPACES ONLINE

The internet is home to negative things like hackers, cyberbullies, and inappropriate content. But with the right skills, you can learn how to use it safely and positively. After all, the internet is meant to be a tool for finding information, learning new things, expressing yourself, and connecting with others! It's possible to create safe spaces online so you can do all of those things.

YOUR PRIVACY

Protecting your privacy is one of the best things you can do to stay safe online. Ask yourself: Do I even need or want a social media profile right now, and if I do, how can I keep it private and safe?

You may want to use only your first and middle name on social media accounts, or a nickname. Some social media accounts make it possible for you to block others from finding you, so you have control over who can see that you even have an account. You can block people from contacting you on almost all social networks. This cuts off access to you so they can no longer contact you or see what you post. You can also block people over email and cell phone. Check into your account settings to add blocks.

You can choose what you want the public to view and what you want your friends to view. On some websites, such as Facebook, you can keep information private for certain friends while allowing others to view your whole page. Check the privacy settings of your social media accounts regularly as they sometimes change.

POST MINDFULLY

Sometimes people post without thinking, often because they're excited, sad, angry, or annoyed. To create a safe space for yourself online, think before you post anything emotional.

Never post anything online or send anything through text that you wouldn't want everyone to see. This may sound unfair. What if you have a picture you just want to send to your boyfriend or girlfriend? What if you want to tell someone a secret via text?

Always be on your guard about what you send. If you want to protect yourself against future embarrassments, never send sexual pictures of yourself to anyone over the internet. Once they're created and sent, they can never be taken back.

Keep your language online kind and considerate. Keep your photographs appropriate. Ask yourself: Would I want my teacher to read this post? Would I want my parents to see this picture?

Refrain from using violent, discriminatory, or biased language online unless you want that image of you to live on forever. You could also be charged with harassment or cyberhate. Don't post anything in anger, desperation, or revenge, as it can be used against you and may hurt others.

You can't control what others say about your social media profile or posts. However, you *can*

control the tone and content you decide to put out into the world. If you feel good about what you're posting, then you might feel more validated or resilient when cyberbullies come around.

SHUT CYBERBULLYING DOWN!

You have the power to shut cyberbullying down when you see it happen. There are many roles in play during a cyberbullying attack, and each person has the power to stop the whole thing.

Have you ever been a cyberbully? Maybe you didn't mean to hurt someone, but you still posted something negative or engaged in a fight in the comments section. When you are the bully, you have the greatest responsibility to end the violence. You can make the active choice to recognize the pain you've caused others, to apologize, and to stop bullying in the future.

Have you ever been an accomplice or reinforcer, someone who gives support and attention to a cyberbully? Accomplices may forward or like a post or picture, may help spread lies and rumors, and may start sending rude comments themselves. If you recognize that you're an accomplice to a cyberbully, remove your support from the bully. Refuse to harass a person just because other people are doing it.

86 I AM BEING CYBERBULLIED...WHAT'S NEXT?

Cyberbullies gain many accomplices because the internet allows so many people to spread and comment on hurtful posts.

CREATING SAFE SPACES ONLINE

You may receive a text with a picture of someone and be told to pass it on. In that moment, you have to choose: Do you want to be an accomplice or break the cycle of bullying? If you don't send the picture or post on, then it won't reach as many people, and it may stop with you.

Have you ever been a bystander, watching in the wings as someone bullies another person online? This happens often online because many young people believe that writing hurtful posts about someone else is normal. A person might be afraid that by doing something, they might be the next target. However, by being a bystander, you're allowing the cyberbullying to keep happening.

The best role to play in a cyberbullying situation is the defender. Next time you see someone cyberbullying another person, you can report the bullying anonymously. Many schools accept anonymous tips about bullying. You can also report the mean or hurtful posts to the social media website. The cyberbully never needs to know that it was you who turned them in. You can even try reasoning with the cyberbully, though sometimes they can be easily provoked.

LET'S DITCH THE LABELS

In this book, we've used the terms "bully" and "victim" quite often. Though those labels are convenient when talking in general, it's important to remember that in real life, people are more than just those labels.

A "bully" usually has something else going on in their life that leads them to act that way. They may actually be a victim at home or in another social situation. They may have poor coping skills, low self-esteem, or mental health issues. They may be acting out of revenge for some hurt that was done to them. One person might think they're a victim, when really they have bullied others too.

Using labels also creates a fixed mindset—or the thought that someone can't change—rather than a growth mindset, or the thought that people *can* change. The person who is bullying you might develop coping skills or mature as they grow older. Cruel behavior is never acceptable, but using empathy toward both "bullies" and "victims" can help create a more understanding environment online.

You can help break a cycle of cyberbullying by speaking up and supporting the person being bullied.

If talking to the cyberbully or reporting them doesn't work, try to reach out to the victim. The victim may feel isolated and alone. They may have low self-esteem and feel that no one cares about them. By reaching out and letting them know you're on their side, you can make someone feel better and stronger.

If you're the victim, don't be afraid to reach out for help. You have nothing to be ashamed of, even if a cyberbully is shaming you with pictures and secrets. Recognize that you have the power to break the cycle too—even if the cyberbully makes you feel powerless.

You have the power to make your school and online community into a safer, more respectful place to be.

CHANGE THE TONE!

Do you feel like social media has become a place of negativity and hate? Do you feel like people mostly use it to fight and bully? It's time to change the tone! Be a role model of kindness through your words and actions. The way you act may inspire others to act with kindness too.

You can also raise awareness about cyberbullying through social media posts, conversations with school leaders, and talks with friends. By getting the word out there, you're opening up conversations between people, so maybe victims can open up about their experiences and bullies can learn from them. A school community that communicates is one in which people understand each other. The antidote for bullying is understanding and kindness.

Spread the word about antibullying campaigns such as STOMP Out Bullying, which leads a #seeme campaign and a National Block It Out Day to raise awareness of cyberbullying. Educate people on kindness campaigns, such as Random Acts of Kindness (randomactsofkindness.org), The Kindness Campaign (tkckindness.org), and Rachel's Challenge (rachelschallenge.org). Changing the tone of online interactions from one of aggression and hate to one of kindness and understanding can do more than just change your own experience—it can save a life.

CONCLUSION

When cyberbullying happens, it can feel inescapable. You might feel powerless, as if you have no way to deal with the negative emotions and hateful attacks you're facing. But developing coping skills and interpersonal skills can help you to overcome the situation—and even grow from it.

Your voice matters. If cyberbullying is happening to you, don't suffer in silence. Reach out, advocate for your rights, and create a safe space for yourself—in real life and online.

CYBER
BULLYING

GLOSSARY

aggressive: Ready or likely to attack or confront.
alleged: Accused but not yet proven or convicted.
blackmail: Demanding money or services from a person in return for not revealing compromising information for that person.
confidential: Entrusted with private information; intended to be kept secret.
default: To automatically go back to a preselected option.
elusive: Hard to get.
emotional intelligence: The ability to identify and manage one's own emotions, as well as the emotions of others.
empathy: The ability to understand and feel another person's feelings.
exacerbate: To make a situation worse.
explicit: Depicting nudity or sexuality.
forge: To fake something to trick someone.
harass: To repeatedly annoy, bother, or attack someone.
impersonate: To pretend to be someone else.
inadequate: Not enough or not good enough.
incriminate: To make someone appear guilty of a crime or wrongdoing.
manipulate: To control or influence someone unfairly.
mantra: A saying that is meant to bring up a certain feeling, wish, or intention.

offensive: Causing displeasure or resentment.

prevalence: The quality or state of being widely accepted or practiced.

recruit: To increase the number of something with new members.

resilience: The ability to recover or adjust from misfortune or change.

stalk: To follow, watch, and bother someone constantly in a way that seems threatening or dangerous.

transgender: Of or relating to a person who has a gender identity that differs from the person's assigned sex at birth (for example, a person is born assigned male but identifies as female).

trauma: A very unpleasant or difficult experience that causes someone emotional or mental problems for a prolonged period of time.

validate: To recognize, establish, or illustrate the worthiness or legitimacy of something, especially a thought or feeling.

victim blaming: The attitude that suggests that a victim is responsible for the wrong that is done to them.

visualize: To form a mental image of something.

vulnerable: Capable of being physically, mentally, or emotionally wounded.

FOR MORE INFORMATION

Cyberbullying Research Center
Website: cyberbullying.us
Facebook and Instagram:@cyberbullyingresearch
Twitter: @onlinebullying
The Cyberbullying Research Center is an online collection of the latest data on cyberbullying, with real-life information and guidance on how it affects young people. Run by Drs. Justin W. Patchin and Sameer Hinduja, this website provides resources for parents, educators, counselors, and others who work with youth.

The Cybersmile Foundation
99 Hudson Street 5th Floor
New York, NY 10013
Website: www.cybersmile.org
Facebook: @TheCybersmileFoundation
Twitter: @CybersmileHQ
Instagram: @cybersmilefoundation
The Cybersmile Foundation is a nonprofit organization that fights against cyberbullying by promoting kindness and positivity online. It runs a research center and antibullying campaigns and hosts a Stop Cyberbullying Day for global unity and positivity online.

Dare to Care

+1 403-620-5156
Website: www.daretocare.ca
Facebook: @daretocare
Twitter and Instagram: DareToCare2
Dare to Care is a comprehensive bully prevention program in Canada. It helps schools, communities, and sports teams foster a caring community through programs, workshops, and resources.

End to Cyber Bullying Organization

60 W 38th St, Floor 2
New York, NY 10018
1-772-202-ETCB (3822)
Website: www.endcyberbullying.org
Facebook: @endtocyberbullying
Twitter: @ETCBtweet
End to Cyber Bullying (ETCB) is a nonprofit organization that encourages teens to be the change online. It provides essential cyberbullying information and is available for teens to reach out to if they are experiencing cyberbullying.

PACER's National Bullying Prevention Center

80 E. Hillcrest Drive, #203
Thousand Oaks, CA 91360
952.838.9000 or 800.537.2237
Website: www.pacer.org/bullying
 /resources/cyberbullying/
Facebook: @PACERsNationalBullying
 PreventionCenter
Twitter and Instagram: PACER_NBPC
PACER's National Bullying Prevention Center is committed to leading social change to prevent childhood bullying. Resources for students, parents, and educators can be found on its website and social media platforms.

PREVNet

PREVNet Administrative Centre
Queen's University
100 Barrie Street
Kingston, ONcK7L 3N6
Tel : (613) 533-2632
Toll Free: (866) 372-2495
Website: www.prevnet.ca
Facebook, Twitter, and Instagram: @PREVNet
PREVnet is Canada's healthy relationships hub—a national network of organizations and researchers committed to preventing bullying. PREVnet's website provides the latest information and resources for teens, parents, and educators about bullying and cyberbullying.

STOMP Out Bullying
877 NoBULLY (877 602 8559)
Website: www.stompoutbullying.org
Facebook and Twitter: @StompOutBullying
Instagram: @theofficialstompoutbullying
STOMP Out Bullying is a national nonprofit that works to reduce and prevent bullying and cyberbullying. It provides effective solutions to bullying situations, and its help line is available to all young people who are being bullied. The free and confidential help line is staffed with nonjudgmental volunteers.

The Trevor Project
1-866-488-7386
Website: thetrevorproject.org
Facebook: @TheTrevorProject
Twitter and Instagram: @trevorproject
Founded in 1998, the Trevor Project aims to provide resources and crisis prevention for LGBTQ+ teens. It provides a 24-hour chat service, text support, and phone line for young people who need help.

FOR FURTHER READING

Biram, Tracy. *Cyberbullying*. Cambridge, UK: Independence Educational Publishers, 2019.

Gagne, Tammy. *Online Shaming and Bullying*. San Diego, CA: ReferencePoint Press, 2019.

Gordon, Sherri M. *Weaponized Social Media*. New York, NY: Enslow Publishing, 2019.

Hitchcock, J.A. *Cyberbullying at the Wild, Wild Web*. Lanham, MD: Rowman and Littlefield, 2019.

Mapua, Jeff. *Coping with Cyberbullying*. New York, NY: Rosen Publishing, 2018.

MacCarald, Clara. *Beating Bullying at Home and in Your Community*. New York, NY: Rosen Publishing, 2018.

Miller, Derek L. *Dealing with Cyberbullying*. New York, NY: Cavendish Square Publishing, 2019.

Miller, Marie-Thérèse. *Teens and Cyberbullying*. San Diego, CA: ReferencePoint Press, 2020.

Patchin, J. W. & Hinduja, S. *Words Wound: Delete Cyberbullying and Make Kindness Go Viral*. Minneapolis, MN: Free Spirit Publishing, 2014.

Rusick, Jessica. *#IAmAWitness: Confronting Bullying*. Minneapolis, MN: Abdo Publishing, 2020.

Sherer, Lauri S. *Cyberbullying*. New York, NY: Greenhaven Press, 2015.

Subramanian, Mathangi. *Bullying: The Ultimate Teen Guide*. Lanham, MD: Rowman and Littlefield, 2017.

The New York Times Editorial Staff. *Cyberbullying: A Deadly Trend*. New York, NY: New York Times Educational Publishing, 2019.

INDEX

A
anxiety, 40, 44, 45, 46, 48, 49, 52, 56, 67, 69, 73, 75, 79

C
catfishing, 19, 20
cyber self-harm, 52

D
depression, 40, 44, 48, 49, 52, 56, 67, 69, 73, 79
discrimination, 58, 59, 63

F
Facebook, 4, 10, 17, 18, 43, 83

G
gender identity, 12, 14, 60

H
hate crime, 60
hate speech, 13

I
Instagram, 4, 5, 10, 17, 29, 46

L
LGBTQ+ youth, 12

P
photographs/pictures, 4, 6, 9, 10, 16, 18, 20, 22, 23, 24, 25, 27, 28, 29, 30, 31, 32, 33, 34, 35, 37, 38, 45, 46, 68, 73, 80, 83, 84, 85, 87, 90

R
revenge porn, 38

S
self-esteem, 29, 43, 44, 46, 69, 71, 76, 88, 89
self-harm, 49, 50, 51, 52
sexting, 38, 58, 61
sextortion, 61
sexual orientation, 12, 13, 14, 59, 60
Snapchat, 4, 10, 17
social anxiety, 46, 47
social media, 4, 8, 9, 10, 13, 16, 17, 24, 29, 52, 54, 59, 71, 77, 82, 83, 84, 88, 91
substance abuse, 52, 53, 54
suicide, 30, 49, 50, 51, 52, 54, 55, 56, 57

T
threats, 6, 11, 13
TikTok, 4, 5, 10, 51
Tumblr, 4
Twitter, 10, 17

Y
YouTube, 4, 17

ABOUT THE AUTHOR

C. R. McKay is a writer and editor from Buffalo, NY. She is the author of many fiction and nonfiction books for kids and teens, including several guidance books on social and emotional learning skills and anxiety disorders. She believes in the power of kindness and mindfulness, both online and in person. As someone who has suffered from anxiety disorders in her own life, she hopes to instill a message of hope and resilience in her young readers, and wants them to know—it gets better.

CREDITS

Photo Credits: Cover, p. 9 Richard Bailey/Corbis/Getty Images; Cover, pp. 1–104 LUMIKK555/Shutterstock.com; Cover, pp.1–104 Filin84/Shutterstock.com; p. 5 SDI Productions/E+/Getty Images; p. 7 Prostock-studio/Shutterstock.com; p. 10 Mayur Kakade/Moment/Getty Images; p. 12 praetorianphoto/E+/Getty Images; p. 16 Elitsa Deykova/E+/Getty Images; p.19 Pixel-Shot/Shutterstock.com; p. 21 Yagi Studio/DigitalVision/Getty Images; p. 23 AleksandarGeorgiev/E+/Getty Images; p. 26 Pornsawan Sangmanee/EyeEm/Getty Images; pp. 28, 40 martin-dm/E+/Getty Images; pp. 31, 39 Africa Studio/Shutterstock.com; p. 32 MStudioImages/E+/Getty Images; p. 35 Syda Productions/Shutterstock.com; p. 36 William Perugini/Image Source/Getty Images; p. 42 ljubaphoto/E+/Getty Images; p. 45 Peter Dazeley/The Image Bank/Getty Images; pp. 47, 62 FatCamera/E+/Getty Images; p. 51 NurPhoto/Contributor/Getty Images; p. 53 Jack Andersen/DigitalVision/Getty Images; p. 55 Justin Paget/Stone/Getty Images; p. 57 Sabphoto/Shutterstock.com; p. 59 Deepak Seth/E+/Getty Images; p. 65 DGLimages–/Shutterstock.com; p. 67 Maskot/Getty Images; p. 70 Jun Sato/TAS18/Contributor/Getty Images Entertainment/Getty Images; p. 72 Lina Bruins/EyeEm/Getty Images; p. 75 VH-studio/Shutterstock.com; pp. 76, 79 Monkey Business Images/Shutterstock.com; p. 81 GiorgioMagini/Shutterstock.com; p. 84 MStudioImages/E+/Getty Images; p. 86 SolStock/E+/Getty Images; p. 89 Motortion Films/Shutterstock.com; p. 90 Jon Feingersh Photography Inc/The Image Bank/Getty Images; p. 93 Lucky Business/Shutterstock.com; p. 94 Makistock/Sutterstock.com; p. 95 Rawpixel.com/Shutterstock.com.